W9-ASN-962

GRAPHIC PREHISTORIC ANIMALS

SABERTOOTH TIGER

SMILODON

ILLUSTRATED BY ALESSANDRO POLUZZI

A⁺

Smart Apple Media

Published by Smart Apple Media, an imprint of Black Rabbit Books
P.O. Box 3263, Mankato, Minnesota 56002
www.blackrabbitbooks.com

Produced by David West 大大 Children's Books
6 Princeton Court, 55 Felsham Road, London SW15 1AZ

Designed and written by Gary Jeffrey

Copyright © 2017 David West Children's Books

Library of Congress Cataloging-in-Publication Data

Names: Jeffrey, Gary, author. | Poluzzi, Alessandro, illustrator.
Title: Sabertooth tiger / written by Gary Jeffrey ; illustrated by Alessandro
   Poluzzi.
Other titles: Saber tooth tiger
Description: Mankato, Minnesota : Smart Apple Media, [2017] | Series: Graphic prehistoric animals | Audience: K to
grade 3._ | Includes index.
Identifiers: LCCN 2015036960| ISBN 9781625884114 (library binding) | ISBN 9781625884275 (ebook)
Subjects: LCSH: Saber-toothed tigers–Juvenile literature. | Saber-toothed
   tigers–Comic books, strips, etc. | Mammals, Fossil–Juvenile literature.
   | Mammals, Fossil–Comic books, strips, etc. | CYAC: Prehistoric animals.
   | LCGFT: Graphic novels.
Classification: LCC QE882.C15 W47 2017 | DDC 569.7–dc23
LC record available at http://lccn.loc.gov/2015036960

Printed in China
CPSIA compliance information: DWCB16CP
010116

9 8 7 6 5 4 3 2 1

CONTENTS

WHAT IS A SABERTOOTH TIGER?

SMILODON MEANS "BLADE TOOTH"

Sabertooths lived around 2.5 million to 10,000 years ago, during the **Pleistocene period**. **Fossils** of their skeletons have been found in North America and South America (see page 22).

🐾 It had a pair of very long **canine** teeth that curved like a saber sword.

🐾 Its shoulders, front legs, and neck were massively powerful—much stronger than a modern-day lion.

🐾 Although slightly smaller, it was twice as heavy as a lion.

🐾 Its jaws could open twice as wide as a lion's.

🐾 Its short tail shows it might not have chased its prey over long distances in the way a lion does.

SMILODON FATALIS (DEADLY) MEASURED 5.7 FEET (1.74 M) LONG AND 3.3 FEET (1 M) HIGH AT THE SHOULDER. IT WEIGHED 620 POUNDS (281 KG).

🐾 It had strong, short back legs for jumping.

🐾 Its powerful claws could be pulled in and held inside its large paws.

This would be a sabertooth tiger and you.

SABERTOOTH FACTS

During the last big ice age, camels, giant bison, and huge mammoths roamed all across North America. These massive **herbivores** were preyed on by powerful **carnivores,** such as big cats, wolves, and giant bears. Of all these mega carnivores, the strong sabertooth, with its fearsome fangs, was the best equipped to ambush and kill big game quickly.

Smilodon's daggerlike canines measured 7 inches (17.8 cm) long. They were saw–toothed on both edges to slice through flesh easily. Strong when pulled from front to back, they were surprisingly **fragile** if pulled from side to side and could snap. A sabertooth had to be very careful how it caught its prey.

Smilodon had curved saberteeth to slide in and out of flesh for a killing blow…

…front teeth for carving

…and side teeth for biting off lumps of flesh for swallowing.

It is thought sabertooths might have cared for sick or injured members of their group, like African lions do today.

SABERTOOTH ON THE NORTH AMERICAN PLAINS

WHAT IS NOW CALIFORNIA, 30,000 YEARS AGO.

SHEAR TOOTH, THE **ALPHA MALE** OF A GROUP OF SABERTOOTHS, WATCHES AS HIS FEMALES CREEP TOWARD A GIANT BISON THAT HAS STRAYED TOO CLOSE TO THE TREES.

THEY NEED TO GET WITHIN STRIKING DISTANCE. IF THE PREY STARTS TO RUN, IT COULD BE IMPOSSIBLE TO CATCH.

FOR NOW, THE YOUNG BISON DOESN'T KNOW THE STALKERS ARE WATCHING.

SHEAR TOOTH LOST HALF OF ONE OF HIS HUGE CANINE TEETH IN A STRUGGLE WITH A MAMMOTH, BUT HE CAN SURVIVE WITHOUT IT. THE FEMALES DO THE HUNTING FOR HIM.

THE LONG GRASS AND SHRUBS GIVE EXCELLENT COVER FOR THE AMBUSH. TWO FEMALES CLOSE IN. THE BISON'S FINAL MOMENTS APPROACH.

THE REAR FEMALE COILS HER SHORT, POWERFUL BACK LEGS AND LEAPS.

THE STARTLED BISON BOLTS AS SHE CLAWS AT ITS REAR END...

GRAAAAAGH!

MWAAAAGH!

...BUT FAILS TO HOOK ON.

ANOTHER FEMALE LEAPS AT THE BISON AND HOLDS IT IN A DEATH GRIP. USING HER IMMENSE UPPER BODY STRENGTH, SHE WRESTLES IT DOWN TO THE GROUND.

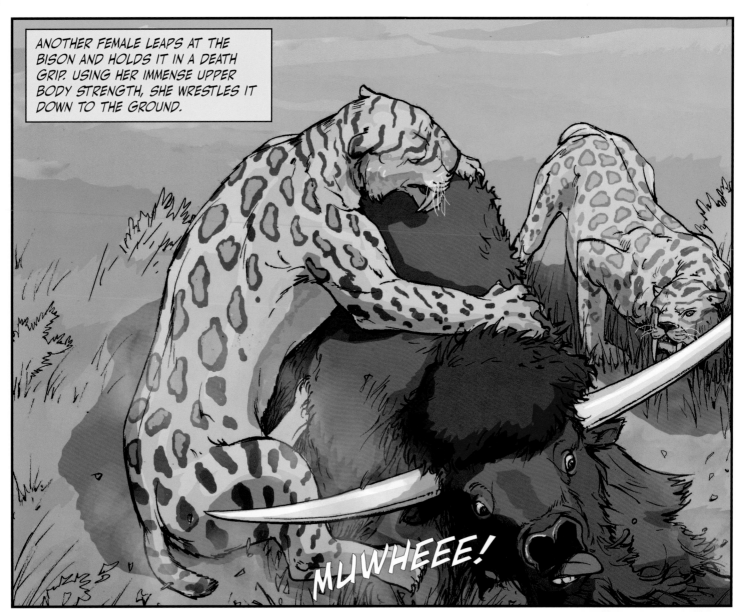

MUWHEEE!

THE OTHER FEMALE POUNCES, THIS TIME HOOKING HER *SWORDLIKE* CLAWS FIRMLY INTO FLESH.

GRAAAAGH!

THE BISON IS *PINNED*.

A THIRD FEMALE EMERGES FROM THE GRASS. SHE WAS WAITING FOR HER MOMENT TO ACT.

GRAAAAGH!

MWHEEEEEEEEEEEEEEEE

CAREFULLY POSITIONING HERSELF IN FRONT OF THE STRUGGLING BISON'S THROAT...

...SHE PLUNGES IN HER CANINES AND BITES BACK.

GRRRRR

SHE QUICKLY PULLS OUT HER SABERTEETH.

THE BISON WILL BE DEAD IN SECONDS.

ROARS FROM THE FEMALES DRAW THE FAMILY GROUP IN TO FEED. SPACE IS MADE FOR SHEAR TOOTH TO TAKE HIS PICK FROM THE BEST PARTS OF THE **CARCASS.**

REEOW!

GROUAAAAGH!

THEY EAT ONLY THE SOFTEST BODY PARTS. THE CATS' SABERTEETH ARE TOO FRAGILE TO RISK BITING ON BONE.

THEY MUST EAT QUICKLY. THE STRONG SMELL OF BLOOD FROM THE KILL IS ATTRACTING THE ATTENTION...

...OF OTHERS.

SNORT-SNUFFLE

GRRRRRR!

10

A GIANT SHORT-FACED BEAR BURSTS FROM THE TREES, SCENTING THE KILL SITE. IT RISES TO ITS FULL HEIGHT AND BELLOWS ITS CLAIM TO THE KILL.

BROUUHAAAA!

THE HUGE BEAR NOW HAS THE ADVANTAGE. THE SABERTOOTHS DARE NOT RISK THEIR TEETH BY BITING IT, AND THEIR PAWS ARE NO MATCH FOR THE BEAR'S FEARSOME CLAWS.

ALL THE TIGERS BUT SHEAR TOOTH BACK OFF. STILL FEEDING, HE ROARS IN REPLY...

GRAAAAAAA!

...BUT IS SUDDENLY DISTRACTED.

11

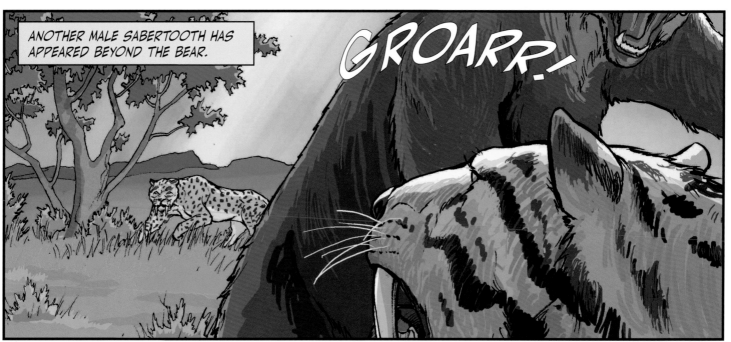

ANOTHER MALE SABERTOOTH HAS APPEARED BEYOND THE BEAR.

GROARR!

THE BEAR SUDDENLY SWIPES AT SHEAR TOOTH, BATTING HIM SIDEWAYS.

RARGH!

SCRITCH!

AROUUUUUGH!

SHEAR TOOTH IS WOUNDED. HE LIMPS AWAY AFTER HIS GROUP AS BIRDS CIRCLE, WAITING FOR THE BEAR TO FINISH WITH THE BISON.

THE STRANGE MALE, MARKED WITH A DISTINCTIVE WHITE FLASH ACROSS HIS FACE, BOUNDS PAST SHEAR TOOTH TO GET AHEAD OF HIM.

HE BLOCKS SHEAR TOOTH'S ROUTE TO HIS GROUP AND ROARS A CHALLENGE.

ROAAAARRR!

SOME OF SHEAR TOOTH'S RIBS ARE CRACKED, AND HIS LEG IS DAMAGED. HE CAN'T FIGHT THIS RIVAL. HE TURNS AWAY.

ROAAAR!

WHITE FLASH APPROACHES THE FEMALES. THEY SNARL AT HIM TO KEEP HIS DISTANCE. THEY WILL NOT ACCEPT HIM UNTIL THE CUBS FATHERED BY SHEAR TOOTH HAVE GROWN.

ROAAAR!
REEEE!

IF HE GETS CLOSE TO THE CUBS, HE MIGHT EAT THEM.

WEEKS LATER, ALTHOUGH HIS WOUNDS ARE SLOWLY HEALING, SHEAR TOOTH IS IN WORSE SHAPE.

HE HAS BECOME AN UNDERWEIGHT WANDERER WHO IS CONSTANTLY HUNGRY. ALTHOUGH WARM, THE WEATHER HAS BEEN WET, AND SHEAR TOOTH CANNOT FIND ENOUGH FOOD.

APPROACHING A CAMEL KILLED BY A PRIDE OF AMERICAN LIONS, HE WAS DRIVEN OFF BY THE ALPHA MALE. A PACK OF DIRE WOLVES WERE WAITING IN THE WINGS, READY TO TAKE OVER ONCE THE LIONS HAD FINISHED.

RAAAAGH!

SHEAR TOOTH HAD TO FIGHT WITH A VULTURELIKE TERATORN FOR THE MORSELS THE WOLVES LEFT BEHIND.

14

SMALLER GAME, LIKE THE DWARF PRONGHORN, ARE PLENTIFUL, BUT THE SABERTOOTH IS NOT BUILT FOR HIGH-SPEED CHASES.

THE SMALLEST PREY, LIKE RABBITS AND PECCARIES, ARE NOT A BIG MEAL AND ARE HARD TO EAT WITH OVERSIZED CANINES.

GRAAANYAAAGH!

THE TIGER'S OUTLOOK IS BLEAK.

EARLY ONE EVENING, WHILE SEARCHING FOR WATER, SHEAR TOOTH'S EARS PICK UP THE DISTANT SOUND OF AN ANIMAL CRYING IN DISTRESS.

REEW! REEW! REEE

HE HEADS TOWARD THE DIRECTION OF THE NOISE. A TRAPPED OR WOUNDED ANIMAL MIGHT MEAN AN EASY MEAL.

REEW! REEW! REEEW! REEW! REEW!

A COLUMBIAN MAMMOTH LIES STRANDED IN THE MIDDLE OF A SHALLOW, BOGGY POND.

IT HAD BEEN TRYING TO REACH A GROUP OF YOUNG TREES IN THE MIDDLE OF THE WATER.

BRUUUAAAGH! REEW! REEW! REEW! REEW! REEW!

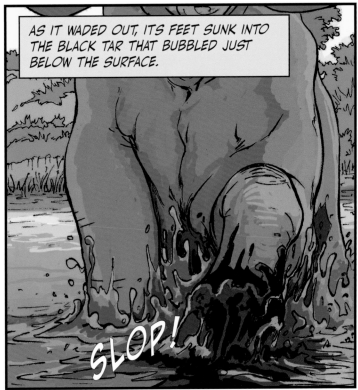

AS IT WADED OUT, ITS FEET SUNK INTO THE BLACK TAR THAT BUBBLED JUST BELOW THE SURFACE.

SLOP!

THE TAR WORKED JUST LIKE GLUE.

BRUUAAAAGH!

16

SHEAR TOOTH DOESN'T KNOW THAT THE POND IS A HIDDEN DEATH TRAP.
THE MAMMOTH'S CRIES GET FAINTER AS IT BECOMES EXHAUSTED.

APART FROM A LURKING BOBCAT, THE
SABERTOOTH IS THE ONLY MAJOR
PREDATOR ON THE SCENE.

SHEAR TOOTH REACHES OUT A
PAW TO ENTER THE BOG WHEN...

RAAAAGH!

WHITE FLASH STANDS WITH THE SABERTOOTH CLAN. THEY, TOO, HAD HEARD THE MAMMOTH'S CRIES.

RAAAAGH!

GROOUUGH!

HE SNAPS AT SHEAR TOOTH TO BACK AWAY.

RAAAAGH!

THIS PREY WILL BE HIS TO CLAIM.

ROAAAR!

THE FEMALES AND CUBS LOOK ON AS WHITE FLASH ENTERS THE WATER.

GRRRRRRRRR!

HIS POWERFUL LEGS TAKE HIM HALF WAY TO THE MAMMOTH...

...BUT NO FARTHER.

RAAAAGH?

HIS FEET ARE CLAMPED FIRMLY IN **ASPHALT**. THIS **TAR SEEP** WILL BE HIS TOMB.

ROOOOOOOOO...

SHEAR TOOTH RETURNS TO THE WATER'S EDGE. HE SNAPS AT THE FEMALES TO GET BACK.

GRAAAGH!

GRRRR!

GRRRR!

ZZZZZT

A WHOLE MAMMOTH IS TOO GOOD TO RESIST.

AGAIN HE PREPARES TO ENTER THE POND.

AWROOOUGH!
AWROOOUGH!

A NOISE FROM THE TREE LINE, GETTING LOUDER AND LOUDER, MAKES HIM HESITATE.

A HUGE PACK OF MARAUDING DIRE WOLVES ADVANCES TOWARD THE SABERTOOTHS.

WHILE THE BOLDEST WOLVES BARK AT THE SABERTOOTHS, THEIR PACK MATES RUSH INTO THE WATER.

AWROOOUGH!

HEAVILY OUTNUMBERED, THE CLAN RETREATS WITH SHEAR TOOTH CLOSE BEHIND.

AWROOOOOOO

THE FEMALE GROUP NOW HAS NO MALE. THE FEMALES MIGHT MAKE SPACE FOR SHEAR TOOTH AT THE NEXT KILL. THEN THEY MIGHT LET HIM HEAD THEIR GROUP ONCE MORE.

FOSSIL FINDS

WE CAN GET A GOOD IDEA OF WHAT **ANCIENT ANIMALS** MAY HAVE LOOKED LIKE FROM THEIR FOSSILS. FOSSILS ARE FORMED WHEN THE HARD PARTS OF AN ANIMAL OR PLANT BECOME BURIED AND THEN TURN TO ROCK OVER MILLIONS OF YEARS.

The largest known sabertooth, *Smilodon populator* (destroyer), lived in South America. Its sabers were an amazing 12 inches (30 cm) long. The La Brea Tar Pits in Los Angeles have yielded the most fossil finds of the sabertooth. Many show healed injuries, and some have broken teeth. Hunting big game was rough work.

Smilodon populator

Both the North and South American sabertooths became extinct at the end of the ice age, along with the giant bear and the American lion. The warming climate may have reduced the rich grasslands, causing the big game to slowly disappear. Unlike coyotes or wolves, sabertooths were not adapted to hunt anything but large, slow-moving animals. They were also poor scavengers. Their heavy build and huge sabers were their undoing.

Smilodon fatalis

ANIMAL GALLERY

All of these **animals** appear in the story.

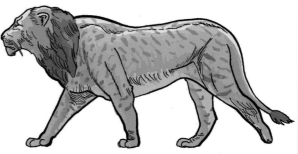

flat-headed peccary
Platygonus compressus
Length: 35 inches (89 cm)
a small mammal similar to a
modern-day wild pig

dire wolf
Canis dirus
Length: 6 ft (1.8 m)
like a modern-day timber wolf
but much heavier

American lion
Panthera atrox
Length: 10 ft (3 m)
like an African lion but with
longer, stronger legs

teratorn
Teratornis merriami
Wing Span: 13 ft (4 m)
a large, condorlike predatory bird with a sharp,
hooked bill for ripping flesh

giant short-faced bear
Arctodus simus
Standing Height: 20–26 ft (6–8 m)
the largest bear ever found; had long legs and
huge bone-crushing jaws

Columbian mammoth
Mammuthus columbi
Overall Length Including Tusks: 28.5 ft (8.7 m)
a primitive elephant with long spiraled tusks

giant bison
Bison latifrons
Length: 15 ft (4.6 m)
larger and heavier than modern-day bison

GLOSSARY

alpha male the highest-ranking member of a group of social animals, such as lions, wolves, and dogs

asphalt an oily mixture of tar and sand

canine a pointed tooth between the front teeth and cheek teeth of a mammal, enlarged for flesh-tearing in meat eaters

carcass the rotting body of a dead animal

carnivore a meat-eating animal

fossils the remains of living things that have turned to rock

fragile easily broken

herbivore a plant-eating animal

marauding roaming with the intention to attack

Pleistocene period the time between 1,640,000 to 10,000 years ago, marked by a series of great ice ages

predator an animal that naturally preys on others

tar seep a sticky pool of oil that bubbles up from the ground

INDEX